CONTENTS

THE FIERY PHOENIX

There is a bird that lays no eggs and has no young. It was here when things began and is still living today, in a hidden, faraway desert place. It is the Phoenix, the bird of fire.

FIERY
PHOENIX
and
The Lemon Princess

Retold by MARGARET MAYO
Illustrated by PETER BAILEY

ORCHARD BOOKS

For Natalie
M.M.
With love to the two young whippersnappers,
Oscar and Felix
P.B.

Orchard Books
96 Leonard Street, London EC2A 4XD
Orchard Books Australia
32/45-51 Huntley Street, Alexandria, NSW 2015
The text was first published in Great Britain in the form
of a gift collection called *The Orchard Book of Magical Tales*
and *The Orchard Book of Mythical Birds and Beasts*
illustrated by Jane Ray, in 1993 and 1996
This edition first published in hardback in 2003
First paperback publication in 2004
The Orchard Book of Magical Tales Text © Margaret Mayo 1993
The Orchard Book of Mythical Birds and Beasts Text © Margaret Mayo 1996
Illustrations © Peter Bailey 2003
The rights of Margaret Mayo to be identified as the author
and Peter Bailey to be identified as the illustrator of this work
have been asserted by them in accordance with the
Copyright, Designs and Patents Act, 1988.
A CIP catalogue record for this book is available from the British Library
ISBN 1 84362 080 4 (hardback)
ISBN 1 84362 088 X (paperback)
1 3 5 7 9 10 8 6 4 2 (hardback)
1 3 5 7 9 10 8 6 4 2 (paperback)
Printed in Great Britain

One day, in the beginning times, the Sun looked down and saw a large bird with the most beautiful shiny feathers. They were red, gold, purple – bright and dazzling like the Sun itself. The Sun called out, "Glorious Phoenix, you shall be my bird and live for ever!"

Live for ever! The Phoenix was really happy when it heard this, and it lifted its head and sang, "Sun, glorious Sun, I shall sing my songs for you alone!"

But the Phoenix was not happy for long.
Poor bird. Its feathers were far too
beautiful. Men, women and children were
always chasing it and trying to trap it.
They wanted to have some of those shiny
feathers for themselves.

'I cannot live here,' thought the Phoenix.
And it flew off towards the east, where the
Sun rises in the morning.

The Phoenix flew
and it flew, until it
came to a faraway,
hidden desert
where there were
no humans. And there
it lived in peace, flying freely and singing
its songs of praise to the Sun above.

Almost five hundred years passed by.
The Phoenix was still alive, but it had
grown old. It was often tired, and it had
lost much of its strength. It couldn't soar
so high in the sky, nor
fly as fast or as far as
when it was young.
'I don't want to live
like this,' thought
the Phoenix. 'I
want to be young
and strong.'

So the Phoenix lifted its head and sang,
"Sun, glorious Sun, make me young and
strong again!" But the Sun didn't answer.
Day after day the Phoenix sang. But
when the Sun still didn't answer, the
Phoenix decided to return to the place
where it had lived in the beginning,
and ask the Sun one more time.

It flew across the desert, and over
hills, green valleys and high mountains.

The journey was long, and because the Phoenix was old and weak, it had to rest on the way. Now the Phoenix has a keen sense of smell, and is particularly fond of herbs and spices. So, each time it landed, it collected pieces of cinnamon bark and all kinds of fragrant leaves. And it tucked some amongst its feathers and carried the rest in its claws.

When the bird came at last to the place which had once been its home, it landed on a tall palm tree that was growing high on a mountainside. Right at the top of the tree, the Phoenix built a nest with cinnamon bark and lined it with the fragrant leaves. Then the Phoenix flew off and collected some of that sharp-scented gum called myrrh, which it had seen oozing out of a tree close by, and made an egg from the myrrh, and carried the egg back to the nest.

Now everything was ready. The Phoenix
sat down in its nest, lifted its head and
sang, "Sun, glorious Sun, make
me young and strong again!"

This time the Sun heard
the song. Swiftly it
chased the clouds
from the sky and
stilled the winds
and shone down on
the mountainside
with all its power.

The animals, the snakes, the lizards and every other bird hid from the Sun's fierce rays, in caves and holes, under shady rocks and trees. Only the Phoenix sat upon its nest and let the Sun's rays beat down upon its beautiful shiny feathers.

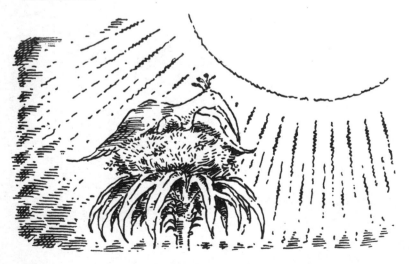

Suddenly there was a flash of light,
flames leapt out of the nest and the
Phoenix became a big round blaze of fire.

After a while the flames died down.
The tree was not burnt, nor was the nest.
But the Phoenix was gone and in the nest
was a heap of silvery-grey ash.

The ash began to tremble and slowly heave itself upward...and from under the ash there rose up a young Phoenix. It was small and looked sort of crumpled. But it stretched its neck and lifted its wings and flapped them. Moment by moment it grew, until it was the same size as the old Phoenix. It looked around and found the egg made of myrrh, hollowed it out, placed the ashes inside and finally closed up the egg.

And then the
Phoenix lifted its
head and sang,
"Sun, glorious
Sun, I shall sing
my songs for
you alone! For
ever and ever!"

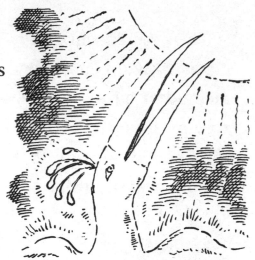

When the song ended, the wind began
to blow, the clouds came scudding across
the sky, and the other living creatures
crept out of their hiding places.

15

Then the Phoenix, with the egg in its claws, flew up and away. At the same time a cloud of birds, of all shapes and sizes, rose up from the earth and flew behind the Phoenix, singing together, "You are the greatest of birds! You are our king!"

And the birds flew with the Phoenix to the temple of the Sun which the Egyptians had built at Heliopolis, City of the Sun. Then the Phoenix placed the egg, with the ashes inside, on the Sun's altar.

"Now," said the Phoenix, "I must fly on alone." And, watched by the other birds, it flew off towards the faraway desert.

The Phoenix lives there still. But every five hundred years, when it begins to feel weak and old, it flies west to the same mountain. There it builds a fragrant nest, on top of a palm tree, and once again it is burnt to ashes. But the Phoenix always rises up from those ashes, fresh and new and young again.

An Egyptian tale

THE LEMON PRINCESS

Once, in the faraway times when toads had wings and camels could fly, there lived a king and queen who had an only son called Prince Omar. A day came when they decided that he must do what every other prince did. He must find a beautiful girl and marry her. So Prince Omar looked for a beautiful wife, *but* – and it was a big *but* – he could not find a girl who was beautiful enough.

Then, one day, an old woman came to him and said, "My lord prince, let me tell you about a princess – an exceedingly beautiful princess – whose face has not yet been seen by the sun. She is the one you seek. She is your fate."

"How can I find her?" he asked.

"You must ride eastwards for three days and three nights," said the old woman, "and then you will come to a garden hedged around with roses, where there grows a lemon tree that bears three ripe lemons. Pick the lemons, but then be careful and do not cut them open until you come to a place where there is plenty of water."

So the next morning Prince Omar mounted his horse and set off. He rode eastwards for three days and three nights, until he came to a garden hedged around with roses. He opened the gate and walked in. He looked all around and he found the lemon tree that had three ripe lemons. So he picked them and rode off, back the way he had come.

Now he had not gone far when he began to wonder what was inside those lemons, so he chose one, took a knife and cut it open. And there rose up from the lemon an exceedingly beautiful girl. "Water!" she called out. "Please give me water!"

But there was no water anywhere, and the next moment the girl faded away and was gone.

Prince Omar was sad. But the thing was done, and there was no going back. So on he rode.

It was not long, however, before he began to wonder about the other two lemons and whether there were girls in them also. So he chose another one, took his knife and cut it open. And there rose up from the lemon a girl who was even more beautiful than the first, and she called out, "Water! Please give me water!"

But again there was no water anywhere, and the girl faded away and was gone.

"I see now that I must take great care of my third lemon," said the prince. And on he rode.

After a while he came to a river, and, remembering the old woman's advice, he took the third lemon and cut it open. And there rose up a girl who was even more beautiful than the two who had come before – eyes gentle as the moon, skin pale as ivory, and hair long, shiny, black and soft as silk. And she too called out, "Water! Please give me water!"

Well, Prince Omar was so anxious not to lose this beautiful girl that he took hold of her and dropped her straight into the river. Just like that. And she drank the clear, fresh water until she was satisfied, and then she climbed out, all naked as she was.

The prince took off his cloak and wrapped it round her. "My beautiful Lemon Princess, you, and you alone, shall be my bride," he said. "But, before I take you to the palace, I must go and fetch some fine clothes for you to wear and a horse for you to ride."

"Then I shall hide in this tall poplar tree, until you return," said the Lemon Princess. And with that she called out, "Bend down, tall tree! Bend down!"

Immediately the tree bent down and she seated herself on the topmost branch, and the tree stood tall again. And then Prince Omar rode off.

Time comes, time goes, and the Lemon Princess sat high in the tree and waited. After a while, a servant girl – an ugly girl, with mean eyes, tangled hair and rough skin – came to fill her water jar at the river. As she bent down, she saw the face of the beautiful Lemon Princess reflected in the clear water.

"There – see how beautiful I am!" she cried. "I always knew I was far too beautiful to be a servant!"

Then she heard someone laugh and a voice call out, "Look up, not down!"

So the servant girl looked up, and when she saw the Lemon Princess sitting at the very top of the poplar tree, she said, "What are you doing up there in that tall tree?"

The Lemon Princess answered, "I am waiting for my bridegroom, the royal prince, to return with fine clothes for me to wear and a horse for me to ride."

Then the servant girl thought some wicked thoughts and she said, "O lady, lovely lady, let me come up and talk to you and help pass the weary hours while you wait."

The Lemon Princess was lonely, so she said, "Bend down, tall tree! Bend down!" And the tree bent down, and the servant girl was soon up amongst the topmost branches.

"O lady, lovely lady," said the servant girl, "who are you with your magic powers? Are you human? Or are you a peri maiden from the land of enchantment?"

The Lemon Princess answered, "I was once a peri maiden, but now I have chosen to enter the world of humans and to become the Lemon Princess."

"O lady, lovely lady, let me comb your long, black hair." And the servant girl began to comb the Lemon Princess's hair and then – she found a hairpin stuck deep in her long, black hair. "O lady, lovely lady, what is this?" she asked.

"It is my talisman," said the Lemon Princess. "Do not touch it." Immediately the servant girl pulled out the hairpin, and *whir-r-r-r!* the Lemon Princess changed into a white dove, fluttered her wings and flew up and away.

Then the servant girl took off her own clothes, threw them into the river below, and they floated away. Then she wrapped the prince's cloak around her and waited.

Now when Prince Omar returned and saw the ugly servant girl in the poplar tree, he was amazed.

"What has happened?" he cried. "You have changed. Your skin is rough and dry."

"It was the sun, my lord," she said. "The scorching sun burnt it."

"But your lips? Your lips that were soft as rosebuds. What about them?"

"It was the wind, my lord," she said. "The hot dry wind cracked them."

"But your eyes that were so large and gentle?"

"It was the tears, my lord," she said. "The tears I wept because I thought you would never return have made them red and swollen."

"But your hair that was soft as silk?"

"It was the black crow, my lord," she said. "The black crow tried to build a nest in my hair and tangled it and made it rough."

Then the ugly servant girl climbed down from the tree and said, "Time is a great healer, my lord. Soon I shall be as I was before."

And Prince Omar believed her. He gave her beautiful clothes to wear – bag trousers, blue as the summer sky, a white silk blouse embroidered with pearls, a jacket of gold thread, gold slippers, a gold head-dress and gold bangles. And then, together, they rode off to the palace.

Well, when Prince Omar took the servant girl to meet the king and queen, they saw at once how ugly she was and they said, "*This* is your chosen bride! Surely not!"

"I have given her my word," said the prince. "And in forty days our marriage shall be celebrated."

Now there was a garden around the king's palace, and every morning a white dove came and sat upon a sandalwood tree and sang. Every day Prince Omar came and stood beneath the tree and listened, and every day he said, "How sad is the song that the white dove sings!"

As soon as the servant girl noticed this, she went to the gardener and said, "The prince commands you to catch the white dove that sings the sad song in the sandalwood tree and kill it and bury it deep in the ground."

And the gardener killed the bird and buried it.

But the next day, at the very place where the dove was buried, there sprang up a great cypress tree, and the wind came and sighed in its branches.

When Prince Omar saw the tree he was astonished. "What wonder is this!" he said. "A cypress where no tree stood before." And when he heard the wind sighing, he said, "How sad is the sound of the wind in its branches!"

Then the servant girl went to the gardener and said, "The prince commands you to cut down the cypress tree and make from its wood a cradle for the son which one day I shall give him. Take any wood that remains and burn it."

And the gardener cut down the tree, and the palace carpenters cut the wood into planks and made a cradle.

Then the gardener gathered all the wood that remained and built a fire. He was just going to throw the last small branch on to the flames, when the  prince's old nurse went by and asked him for some firewood, so he gave her the small branch from the cypress tree.

Now the old nurse put the branch down beside the fireplace in her house, while she went off to market. The moment she shut the door, the branch shivered all over and – well! it changed into a girl. An exceedingly beautiful girl. The Lemon Princess herself.

At once she set to work. She swept the floor. She washed the dishes. She peeled vegetables and cooked a meal. And then she hid behind a door.

When the old nurse returned, she *was* surprised. "Who has done all this?" she said. "A human or one of the peri kind?"

Then the Lemon Princess came out from her hiding place and she said, "I cleaned and I cooked for you, and now, I ask you, will you do something for me? Go to Prince Omar and tell him that there lives in your house a girl who can make fine carpets, and if he will give you silk threads, she will make for him the finest carpet ever seen."

The old nurse went and spoke to the prince, and he ordered that she should be given silk threads and anything else that was needed. So then the Lemon Princess set to work on her carpet.

Time comes, time goes. The day came when Prince Omar was to marry the wicked servant girl. She had not changed. She was as ugly as ever. But the prince said to himself, "Surely she *is* the Lemon Princess – the one who is my fate. Besides, I have given my word, and so I must marry her."

But early in the morning of that very day, the old nurse brought the finished carpet to the prince and said, "My lord, here is a wedding gift!"

Prince Omar unrolled the carpet and he looked. There was a picture of a garden hedged all around with roses, and in the centre of the garden was a portrait of the Lemon Princess.

"Who made this carpet?" asked the prince.

"A girl who lives with me," she answered.

"Bring her to me," he said.

So the Lemon Princess came to the
palace, and the moment Prince Omar saw
her, he knew her.

"Truly," he said, "you alone are my
beautiful Lemon Princess – my fate – the
one who must be my bride. But, tell me,
where have you been? What happened
to you these long and weary days?"

Then the Lemon Princess told him
about the wicked servant girl and all her
evil deeds. And the prince was angry and
sent his guards to find the servant girl.

But as soon as the servant girl heard that she had been discovered, she was up and off, with the guards at her heels. And she kept running until she was over the border and into the next kingdom. Some say she's running still!

But then, at last, there was a wedding, and Prince Omar married the beautiful Lemon Princess. And for seven days and seven nights the pipes were played, the drums rolled and there was feasting, dancing and great merriment.

A Persian tale

THE FIERY PHOENIX

An Egyptian Tale

In *The Fiery Phoenix* this dazzling bird of fire is a symbol of the sun shining through the day, dying at night and rising again each morning. Before we discovered how the solar system works, the sun was a great mystery to everyone and people tried to understand it by making up stories like these. The Australian Aborigines, for example, thought the sun might be a great bonfire in the sky, lit afresh each new day.* In Egypt, the sun can be especially hot and fiery, just like the phoenix in the tale.

Phoenix is the name the Greeks gave to this mythical Egyptian bird. It's original name was *bennu*. Both words mean *palm tree*, so the bird has been named after the tree where it builds its fragrant nest.

Some early writers believed that there really was such a bird. They said it lived east of Egypt, either in Arabia or India. But they disagreed about how long each bird lived. Five hundred years was the favourite choice!

*This story appears in Margaret Mayo's *How the Sun was Made*

THE LEMON PRINCESS

A Persian Tale

Good stories travel, far and wide, and this popular one has been told in many countries from Spain, through to Turkey and Persia (now called Iran). Arabs dominated much of Spain and Portugal for hundreds of years, and they probably brought the story with them. But it seems likely that *The Lemon Princess* started life in Persia as peri maidens, like those in the story, are Persian fairy beings who are beautiful, graceful and kind.

The importance of opening the fruit near water suggests that Prince Omar was travelling across dry, hot desert places. Although the magic fruit varies in different versions of the story, from lemons and oranges to pomegranates and pumpkins, it is always a fruit that flourishes in hot climates.

People all over the world enjoy stories where goodness and true love triumph over evil and selfishness. As in the European tale of *Cinderella*, the Lemon Princess eventually wins her rightful place beside her prince, despite all the attempts to stop her.

MAGICAL TALES
from
AROUND THE WORLD

Retold by Margaret Mayo ✳ *Illustrated by Peter Bailey*

Orchard Myths are available from all good bookshops,
or can be ordered direct from the publisher:
Orchard Books, PO BOX 29, Douglas IM99 1BQ
Credit card orders please telephone 01624 836000
or fax 01624 837033
or e-mail: bookshop@enterprise.net for details.

To order please quote title, author and ISBN
and your full name and address.
Cheques and postal orders should be
made payable to 'Bookpost plc'.
Postage and packing is FREE within the UK
(overseas customers should add £1.00 per book).

Prices and availability are subject to change.